THE GREAT SHAKING

A Richard Jackson Book

THE GREAT SHAKING

An Account of the EARTHQUAKES of 1811 and 1812
by a BEAR Who Was a Witness
New Madrid, Missouri

by JO CARSON

illustrated by ROBERT ANDREW PARKER

ORCHARD BOOKS · NEW YORK

Text copyright © 1994 by Jo Carson
Illustrations copyright © 1994 by Robert Andrew Parker

Orchard Books, 95 Madison Avenue,
New York, NY 10016

Manufactured in the United States of America. Printed by Barton Press, Inc.
Bound by Horowitz/Rae. Book design by Mina Greenstein
The text of this book is set in 15 point ITC Clearface.
The illustrations are hand-colored aquatints reproduced in full color.
1   3   5   7   9   10   8   6   4   2

Library of Congress Cataloging-in-Publication Data
Carson, Jo, date.
The great shaking : an account of the earthquakes of 1811 and 1812 / by a
bear who was a witness, New Madrid, Missouri ; Jo Carson ; illustrated by
Robert Andrew Parker.   p.   cm.
"A Richard Jackson book"—Half t.p.
Summary: A bear who was there describes three earthquakes in Missouri,
in 1811 and 1812, and their aftermath.
ISBN 0-531-06809-9.   ISBN 0-531-08659-3 (lib. bdg.)
[1. Earthquakes—Fiction.   2. Bears—Fiction.]   I. Parker, Robert Andrew, ill.
II. Title.   PZ7.C2388Gr   1994   [E]—dc20   93-4887

To my research associate, Dorothy

—J.C.

To Claudia, Max, Will, Russell, Jack, and Reed

—R.A.P.

The OMENS

In the spring of the year of the great shaking, there were floods. Afterward, the floods were said to be an omen. But here, floods are not unusual in the spring. It rains too much, it floods.

During the summer, people were sick with strange fevers. So it is told. I did not suffer them myself. There were berries ripe, and I was hungry.

It is told that squirrels marched by the tens of thousands to the south. I did not see that either, but afterward, it was told for truth. I do not think squirrels can march. They stop and shake their tails too much to march. They may have felt the changes coming and moved. But marched? I don't think so.

During the fall of the year, there was a comet with two tails in the sky. The comet was still there at the beginning of my time for sleep. It was a winter night when the bother started.

The FIRST EARTHQUAKE

The shakings began as if Mother was rising from her sleep. She sleeps in the winter like I do. Something itched her. I was pushed from my fold in her skin.

There was a sound like thunder but it was not thunder, and Mother's back began to roll in huge waves.

The big old trees leaned with the waves, entangled their upper branches, and came out by the roots in the next wave because they could not let go of one another fast enough. It sounded like they were screaming.

When the waves stopped, Mother had leaks that were not there before, and water rose from them. Horses, cows, and other fools who want leading froze in their tracks and drowned. I swam. It was deep in places. The water was warm, but the weather was cold. It was a hard way to get a bath, but everyone got one, and when we were clean came the holes.

Blows. Thousands of them. They exploded up with steam and dirt for thirty-seven days and nights.

Birds sought comfort in the company of creatures not of their kind. I had six wrens on my back. I saw a stag whose antlers were filled with crows. He did not like the company of crows, but he did not run them off.

White people prayed to their God to spare them. They promised to build churches where there weren't any if they were allowed to live. Sinners rolled on the ground and begged for their souls because they were afraid it was their Judgment Day. It was not.

Red people hoped and prayed this was their Great Spirit moving to make the white people leave their lands and go back where they came from. But it was not.

Black people, many of whom were slaves, thought it might be their God's way to set them free. They too had prayed. It was not that either.

Bears waited because it was not over.

The SECOND EARTHQUAKE

Thisthis time, fissures opened like mouths, and to keep from being swallowed by them, bears and humans climbed onto the fallen trees and held on. For once, we did not try to harm one another. We had a new predator, Mother. She could have eaten us all without so much as a burp when she had finished.

When she had opened all the mouths she wanted, she rolled in waves again, this time like a gentle sea. Thirteen days. I fell when I tried to walk on her back. She hissed and whistled. She thought we were all very funny. There was the sound of wind, but there was no wind. Mother was singing. I sang with her. I sang, "I am not afraid. I am not afraid." But I was.

The THIRD EARTHQUAKE

The thunders grew again. This time, they were so loud that nothing else could be heard, and even Mother was afraid. She trembled.

Clouds of purple dust filled the air, and The Great Bear from the Stars stepped out of the sky onto Mother's back. The footprints were huge. Twenty, thirty acres at a time fell from the weight of them.

The Great Bear from the Stars sat to scratch, and the water in the big river ran backward.

And in the terrible thunders, The Great Bear reminded Mother that some of her children need to sleep in the cold season, and she remembered my kind and stood still again with only a leaning from time to time.

The great shaking was over.

WHAT OF IT?

Bells in church steeples rang as far away as towns on the eastern ocean, and buildings cracked in between, so it is told. I do not know how far away these places are, but I know the eastern ocean is very far.

Mother changed shape here. Places that had been are no more; there are new places. I have not moved; Mother moved, and it does not look the same.

I had to find a new den. Mine was gone. It was a winter of short sleep and bad dreams. I woke up the second time feeling very surly and bearish hungry.

People rebuilt their houses. A few had died, but not many, because there were not many people here and those who were here ran out of their houses before the houses fell. One man died of fright. Some were lost on the big river. Some moved away in search of steadier ground. Those who remained resumed the hunting of bears.

In the spring, the wrens built nests and raised their young and did not mention it. Wrens do not keep history. I do not know about crows, but I doubt if they keep history either.

A Note about Earthquakes

THE PART OF THE EARTH we live on is called the crust. It is harder than the inside of the earth because it is cooler. The inside of the earth is very hot, so hot that it is liquid. We say the inside of the earth, way deep inside, is molten. Between the molten material inside and the hard cool crust outside is a layer scientists say is plastic. That means it is not liquid, but it is not solid either. The crust of the earth floats and moves on this plastic layer.

There are hundreds of pieces of earth's crust, and they have come together in different ways at different times in the earth's history—it is a very, very long history—so that the continents haven't always had the shape they do now. These pieces of the earth's crust are called plates. Sometimes, when plates push together, mountains are made. Sometimes plates split apart and oceans develop between them. All this happens very slowly. But it is happening even as you read this. It never stops.

Sometimes, as the plates push together, one plate slips against the other. This causes the crust of the earth to move. We call the movement an earthquake.

Earthquakes happen all the time, on land and under the ocean. Most of them are so little we can't even feel them. We know they happen because we measure them on instruments that detect movement in the earth. Every day there are thousands of little earthquakes. Big ones don't happen very often.

The three earthquakes the bear talks about were all very big ones. There were visible changes in the surface of the earth over an area the size of the state of Arkansas.

Big earthquakes have aftershocks that are like smaller earthquakes but are caused by the big one. Each of these big earthquakes had aftershocks, which meant the earth was rearranging itself almost constantly for three months.

The epicenter of these earthquakes—the epicenter is the place where the movement in the earth's crust happens—was close to New Madrid, Missouri, so we call these earthquakes the New Madrid Earthquakes. The bear tells what happened at the epicenter of the earthquakes.

Very few people died in these earthquakes because very few people lived close to the epicenter in 1811, and those who did lived in log cabins or other structures that held together long enough to let people get outside. Earthquakes can and do kill people, but it is usually because buildings or bridges collapse or gas lines break and catch fire, not because the earth shakes them to death.